Terry's Tr
The Magician's
Hat

by Mick Gowar

Longman

Terry lay on his bed staring at the ceiling. He couldn't think of anything else to do. He was bored. Bored, bored, bored.

If he'd told any of his friends at school how boring things were at home no one would believe him. They all thought it must be brilliant to live in a hotel where your dad is the boss.

But it wasn't like that. Terry wasn't allowed to help himself to food from the hotel. If he helped himself to a coke from the bar, Mum or Dad said: "No, Terry. That's not for you. It's for the guests."

Everything was for the guests, and it wasn't fair. Terry wasn't allowed to have friends over to swim in the pool because "it's for the guests".

He couldn't have a birthday football party on the lawn because "it might upset the guests."

Other kids moaned that their parents took work home. But for Terry's mum and dad home *was* work, and that meant it was for Terry as well.

"It's no good lying here," Terry
thought. He got off his bed. "If
only I had a dog to take for walks,"
Terry sighed.

"Maybe there'll be something good on
at the cinema. Maybe Mum'll give me next
week's pocket money early," he thought, but
without much hope.

"If only I didn't live in this boring hotel."

Terry went through the white fire door with the Private sign that separated his parents' flat from the rest of the hotel. Mum was coming in the opposite direction.

"What's the matter, Terry?" asked Mum.

"I'm bored," said Terry. "It would be different if I had a dog. I could take it for long walks and …"

"Oh, Terry!" Mum sighed. "We've been through all that. You can't have a dog because of the …"

"I know – because of the guests."

"Some of them are very old. They wouldn't like a dog running round about the hotel. Anyway, I can't discuss it now. You know how busy Saturdays are with all the new guests arriving."

Mum stopped for a moment. She was obviously getting one of her good ideas.

"If you're bored you can help me. I've got to clear out the attic rooms on the top floor. We're going to make them into bedrooms."

"Oh, no!" thought Terry. "More bedrooms means even more guests!"

He followed Mum along the corridor and then up the narrow winding staircase. The corridor at the top of the stairs wasn't carpeted and freshly painted like the ones below. It was dark and dusty and the ceiling was covered with cobwebs.

Mum opened the first door. "We'll start here," she said, switching on the light.

Terry looked round the room. It was even worse than the corridor.

Terry heard the sharp click-clack of heels coming along the bare wooden floor of the corridor.

"Mrs Williams!"

It was Sharon, one of the chambermaids.

"There's a problem with the guest in room 13," said Sharon.

Mum sighed. "There's always a problem with the guest in room 13. You stay here, Terry. I'll be back in a moment."

Terry looked around the room. There was cracked brown lino on the floor. It was stained and chipped and thick with dust.

The room was empty except for an old wardrobe at the far end.

Terry walked slowly across the room towards the wardrobe. He reached out and pulled open the door. There were no clothes in the wardrobe, but there was a large wooden trunk. It was bound with metal strips, like a sea chest.

A faded label was glued to the lid of the trunk. Terry brushed the dust off. On the label was written in old-fashioned, sloping writing:

Lost property: handle with the greatest care

Very carefully Terry lifted the lid. Inside was a jumble of old clothes and other things. There was a pair of baggy leopard-skin shorts, an old silver pocket watch and chain, a long, multi-coloured woollen scarf, and right at the bottom of the heap was a black, silk top hat.

Terry lifted the hat out of the trunk. Around the brim was a black silk ribbon, and tucked into the ribbon was a yellowing piece of paper. Written on the paper was:

This hat belongs to Mr Magico the famous magician.

"Famous?" thought Terry. "I've never heard of him."

He turned the hat over and looked inside it. It didn't look magic. "I wonder if it'll fit me," thought Terry. He put on the hat. It slid down and perched on his ears.

Immediately the hat was on, Terry felt a sharp scratching. "Oh, no!" thought Terry. "It's full of nits!"

He pulled the hat off and two white doves flew out.

"Where did they …?"

But there was no time to think about that. The two terrified birds were flapping madly around the small room.

Terry held out the hat. "Nice birds," he cooed. "Get back in your hat."

But the birds didn't fly politely back into the hat. They shot out of the door. By the time Terry reached the open door, the birds were already at the end of the corridor and flapping down the stairs.

Terry tore after them.
The door at the bottom of the
stairs was shut. The birds were
fluttering. Terry was just creeping
down the stairs after them when the
door at the bottom was suddenly flung
open. It was Sharon.

"Your mum says sorry, but she'll be – aaarrghh!"

Sharon yelled as the birds skimmed over her hair and into the hotel.

"Quick, Sharon! We've got to catch them!" shouted Terry. He rushed towards the great staircase that led to all the downstairs rooms.

As Terry was halfway down the stairs, the hat fell off. A Union Jack, the Stars and Stripes and the Tricolour of France all tumbled out of the hat. They were joined together by a long length of white string.

Out came more and more flags – Germany, Italy, Japan, India – followed by flag after flag that Terry didn't recognise. They were all joined together by the white cord like multi-coloured washing.

They flowed out of the hat and wrapped
themselves around Terry's legs.

Terry wobbled. He tried to keep his balance. Then he tripped, fell over and began to roll faster and faster down the stairs. And as he rolled, the flags wrapped themselves round him like a multi-coloured rug.

Terry hit the bottom step with a bump. The hat rolled into the middle of the entrance hall. As it came to a stop, two enormous white rabbits leapt out and hopped straight through the door … and into the restaurant.

"Maybe nobody will notice," thought Terry, trying to pull the mass of flags from around his legs.

A lot of screams and shouts from the restaurant suggested that the rabbits had been noticed.

Terry tore into the restaurant just in time to see the doves fly out of the open window.

Then there was a bellow from an elderly man who was sitting at a table at the far end of the room.

"Waiter! There's a rabbit in my salad!"

Perched on his plate was one of the rabbits. It was contentedly chomping a lettuce leaf as if it was the most normal thing in the world.

* * * * * * * * * * * *

"There!" said Dad proudly, banging in the last nail. "It looks really international!"

The flags of all nations were now hanging over the top of the bar.

"But, Dad – what are we going to do about the rabbits?"

"Pie?" suggested Dad.

"Oh, Dad, no!"

"Only joking," said Dad. "As soon as I've finished here, Derek the gardener and I are going to build them a hutch. They can live in the garden. They could be very popular with the children who come to stay. They can be your pets – perhaps that'll stop you going on about having a dog."

"Oh, Dad! That's brilliant!"

"But the thing I can't understand, Terry, is where they all came from." Dad looked puzzled. "Rabbits, doves, flags – they don't just appear by magic."

"Well, to tell you the truth, Dad, they did come out of a hat."

"Oh, come off it, Terry …" Dad laughed.

"It's true. Look, I can show you. The hat's still on the floor in Reception."

Terry and his dad walked into Reception. Mum was sitting behind the desk sorting through some papers.

"Okay, Terry, where is it?" asked Dad.

"It's here …" It was Terry's turned to look puzzled.

"Well, it was here."

"Have you seen a hat?" Dad asked Mum.

"A hat?" said Mum. "No. No one's left a hat here."

"But it was ..."

Dad shook his head. "You'll have to do better than that, Terry," he said.

But Terry couldn't think of anything to say.